MALL AMERICAN GIRL

AN AT THE MALL HOLIDAY STANDALONE NOVELLA

SARAH ROBINSON

CHAPTER ONE

KAMAR

"A hot dog eating contest?" Kamar Jaziri frowned as he tried to absorb everything his boss was telling him.

Harold, an older man with thick glasses, shrugged as if he hadn't just tried to strong-arm Kamar into an event he wanted nothing to do with. "Not just hot dogs. There's also the potato sack race and the dunk tank."

Harold was the operations manager at Yule Heights Shopping Mall, and he'd hired Kamar for the summer to play for the evening crowds on Thursday and Friday nights. While the gig wasn't particularly well paid, it was over a holiday weekend and the July Fourth crowd tended to tip nicely. Also thankfully, the pavilion where he'd be performing from was set right outside the entrance to The Lucky Leprechaun, the mall's only bar, so Kamar was hoping some drunk patrons might find their way out and be even more generous with their tips.

But nowhere in his job description had it said anything about potatoes and hot dogs.

He blinked slowly. "And I have to do this *why?*"

"Hey, the majority of this job is the tips." Harold

pointed toward the small stage set up in the center pavilion of the Yule Heights Shopping Mall. "We pay jack shit to our musicians—not my fault, I always try to advocate for more, but the higher-ups run the show. You're going to have to hustle if you want to rake in actual money here, and that means being part of the Yule Heights Independence Games and bumping elbows with vendors who can funnel people your way. How many hot dogs can you eat in a minute?"

Kamar wanted to laugh but he wasn't sure if his new boss had the same sense of humor he did. Was he seriously asking him that question? Or was everyone in this town really into these Independence Games like he said? Being from out of state until recently moving here for college, these weren't exactly the type of festivities he was used to, growing up in New York City. Heck, he couldn't remember the last time he'd even seen a real New Yorker eat a hot dog —that was reserved for tourists and people with iron stomachs.

"Uh, I'm not sure. So, I just need to eat some hot dogs, run a race and that's it?" he asked.

Harold nodded, but then his eyes lit up. "And you have to shoot the deer!"

"Absolutely not." The words came out of Kamar's mouth before he had a chance to try to censor himself. He cringed at the thought of hurting an animal. He was a gentle soul—as his music taste and style made very clear—and murdering Bambi just wasn't on his summer reading list. "Are you telling me that there is hunting involved in this, too?"

Harold laughed—a loud guffaw that tipped his entire head back and made his belly shake. "I hear you loud and clear there, son, but no. That game just involves shooting the fake deer with a soft water pistol to keep them away from your flowers. No real deer involved. You know, my brother was a musician back in the day—rest his soul. Wouldn't hurt a fly, but man would he go to town beating the hell out of some drums."

Kamar grinned at that, though his instrument of choice was acoustic guitar most of the time. He could also play bass and some keyboard, but when he was on stage singing ballads, the acoustic guitar felt the most authentic to him and the message he wanted to portray to the crowd. "Sounds like my kind of guy."

"Your folks live around here?" Harold asked.

Kamar shook his head. "My father's home in New York. He's probably asleep by now—usually snoring by seven on the dot."

"Good man." Harold tipped his chin, nodding his approval. He glanced at his watch, pushing his glasses back up his nose as they slid down. "My Ruth and I are usually the same way. Hence the reason I'm going to head out now so I can get home to her. Let me know if you need anything, but everything should be there."

He pointed one last time toward the pavilion then turned and headed down the main corridor of the mall toward the manager's office at the other end. Kamar looked around him, taking in the different stores facing his small stage—an eyeglasses store called Eye Carumba, Kwik Ink Printing, Summer's Sun Tanning Salon, and the Twisted Bread Pretzel Shop were the closest to him. Somewhere nearby must be a candle store as well, because the scent of flowers and wax was strong in the air.

Certainly not his ideal stage for playing music, but he'd played in worse. And a Master's Degree in music education was not cheap. With the fall semester's tuition already looming heavily on his bank account, he was more than willing to make ends meet however he could.

Kamar got to work on setting up his equipment. There wasn't too much to do except place his combo amplifier next to his microphone stand. He started first with pinning the small banner he'd had printed years ago that he used at all his shows despite the fact that the ink was beginning to fade. He'd had to pay a premium for each color he wanted to use, so he'd scrapped his original idea entirely. It was now just a simple black banner with white letters reading MUSIC LIKE THE MOON and then his contact information below, including a way to tip him directly via Venmo or CashApp.

He tended toward softer ballads and soul-filled songs that he'd written himself, and when he'd combined that with the original meaning of his name in Arabic, it had just seemed right to brand his music under that name. When his mother Djamila had still been living, she'd regularly complimented his crooning style voice and told him that she'd named him after the moon because he was destined to be among the stars.

These days, though, he was beginning to feel less and less like stardom was in his journey.

When the stage was finally aesthetically to his liking, Kamar began plugging in the amp and microphone stand into the outlet on the floor covered by a small, removable grate. He clicked on the amp as soon it was plugged in, but nothing happened. Kamar frowned, then tapped the microphone. Still nothing. Returning to the outlet, he took everything out of the plugs and then put them back in.

Zero power.

Kamar felt his stomach tighten as anxiety swelled in his gut. Thankfully, he had Harold's phone number in his cell so he called him to figure out a solution. But the phone just kept ringing until it went to a message that stated Harold's voicemail was full. Then the line went dead.

"Hey, any chance you know how to get this outlet turned on?" Kamar asked a man walking past the stage who was in maintenance coveralls pushing a mop bucket.

The man removed the headphones in his ears long enough to hear the question, but then put them back in, shrugged his shoulders, and continued walking on.

Kamar surveyed what was around him, but his options were either wait for Harold to answer the phone and miss out on any potential tips in the meantime—or find someone to lend him power.

The bar was not an option since he was worried about drunk patrons tripping over extension cords and suing the pants off him. The pretzel stand next door was completely dark and had a metal gate pulled closed in front of it. The third option was Summer's Sun, a tanning salon that was brighter than any other storefront in the mall.

Bingo!

Unwilling to leave his guitar case unattended, Kamar took it with him as he walked over to the tanning salon. The moment he stepped onto the black-and-white checkered tile floor of the salon, a woman sitting behind the receptionist counter looked up at him with interest.

"Hi, are you the owner?" Kamar placed his hand out between them to introduce himself.

She stood from the chair she'd been sitting in and placed the magazine in her hands on the counter before reaching forward and accepting his hand. "I am. Summer Darby. Are you looking for a tanning service? We also sell packages, if you're considering purchasing for a friend or girlfriend."

He smiled, appreciating that she was going right into sales mode. Clearly, she was a hustler like he was if she owned her own place like this. "Actually, I was wondering if I could ask a favor. One mall vendor to another."

Summer lifted a brow as she waited for him to continue.

"I'm playing out on the pavilion there and need power for my amp. The outlet isn't working, but I have a long extension cord and was hoping to hook it up to your outlet here." He pointed at the outlet by the front door that currently had only one of the two sockets taken. "It'll just be for a few hours and that's it."

She frowned. "I don't know...I pay the electric bill here and it isn't cheap. How many watts is the amp?"

"Ten," he replied. "But I don't want to put you out. What if I hang up a sign by my stand telling people to come in here? You could consider it a marketing expense."

Summer seemed a bit more appeased at that idea. "I guess that could make sense if it actually does bring people in."

She didn't seem fully convinced yet.

"Has it been busy today?" he asked, placing his guitar case on the floor by his feet and leaning against the counter. "I've never actually been in a tanning booth before."

"Spray tan," she corrected and then shook her head. "Well, it's not for everyone. Myself included, of course. I'm as pale as a sheet of paper."

Summer gestured toward her own skin, but Kamar found his gaze traveling down her entire frame slowly. She wasn't the smallest woman, and yet every curve was in the right place. Her clothes were snug, but in a purposeful way, and her shirt cut down just low enough in the front to make him pause there for a second.

"You don't use your own product?" Kamar asked, his

gaze returning to her eyes as he felt his cheeks heat upon realizing he'd just blatantly checked her out. Hopefully she hadn't noticed. That wasn't even his usual behavior since he certainly wasn't interested in romances right now as he was trying to get through graduate school. Something about the way this woman held herself, though...it was intriguing. "Why do you run a tanning salon then?"

"Even if I don't use it often, I'm pretty passionate about giving women an easy and affordable alternative to tanning that is safe for their skin and their health," Summer replied, sitting back down in the chair behind her. "Not enough people take skin cancer and sun safety seriously."

Her last few words sounded strained, and he wanted to ask her more, but it didn't feel like it was his place. Plus, he really did need the power turned on so he could get started earning tips.

"Oh," he replied simply, unsure what else to say. "I hear it'll be pretty sunny this weekend at the Yule Heights Independence Games."

Out of everything in the world, how was that the only thing he could think to say?

But her chin lifted, and her brows were raised when she took in his face. "You're competing in that?"

"Didn't seem to have much of a choice not to," he said with a dry laugh. "Harold seemed pretty insistent."

Her face softened and she smiled. "Harold's a good guy. Old school, but a romantic." She looked at him carefully for another moment, studying his face as if she was looking for something. What that was, he wasn't sure.

Finally, she gestured toward the outlet he'd seen earlier. "The plug is over there. You just need to make sure to tape down the wire so people don't trip over it."

He pushed up to a standing position. "Thank you. I really appreciate it."

"Good luck," she called out to him while he began setting up the extension cord. "I mean, tomorrow at the games."

Kamar grinned. "Are you in it, too?"

"How can I not?" Her smile flattened more into a smug grin, and she wiggled her brows. "After all, I'm the undefeated champion for the last four years running. Wouldn't want anything to change that now."

He stopped in his tracks, turning back to look at her. "You're the undefeated champion...in the hot dog eating contest?"

"If your mind is going somewhere dirty, then you can take a hike," she replied, pointing out into the mall.

Kamar shook his head—*that* thought hadn't crossed his mind. Well, not until right this moment. Jesus, now that mental image was front and center. "No, no, I mean...how many hot dogs did you eat to win last year?"

"It's a sixty second timer, and last year I won with twelve hot dogs." The way she said it so casually was like this was an everyday occurrence. "The year before that, I did eleven."

"In sixty seconds?" he asked again, an incredulous tone seeping into his voice. His gaze swept over her frame again —*where the heck was she putting those hot dogs?* "There's zero chance that's real. Six-zero seconds? Like one single minute?"

"I'll have you know that the world record for ten minutes is seventy-six hot dogs, so it's absolutely possible." Her hands were on her hips now, her chin tilted up just enough so that she could look down her nose at him. "Tomorrow, my goal is thirteen."

He grinned at her. "Well, well, well...never thought I'd say this, but you're going to have some competition this year. I'm going to eat you out."

"What?" Her eyes widened.

"I mean in hot dogs. Like, I'm going to out-eat you. I'm going to eat more hot dogs than you. In the contest." He was stumbling over his words now. *Why the hell had he suddenly lost any semblance of chill around this woman?* "Like as a competitor, in uh, in business. Uh, um, well, I'm going to go start my set. See you tomorrow!"

With that, he turned on his heel and practically ran out of the tanning salon and straight for the pavilion. Flirting, dating...any sort of romantic whim was off the table right now, and he couldn't believe he'd said something so potentially suggestive. That was not like him—his style was romance, not crudeness. Plus, he wasn't in a place in his life where he'd even be able to give attention to a partner—he had to focus on school and earning money for his life post-graduate degree.

That had to be enough for now.

Focus, he reminded himself as he confirmed that the outlet was finally working and he had the power he needed.

Kamar stepped onto the pavilion stage, the guitar against his chest, and breathed the first few words of his song into the microphone...

Under the moonlit palm tree, there was a boy who dreamt of the sun...

CHAPTER TWO

SUMMER

*H*AVE *you seen my favorite green camisole? The one with the tequila bottle on it?*

Winter's name flashed on the screen of Summer's cell phone. And no, the irony was not lost on Summer that her ex-girlfriend's name was Winter.

She wanted to immediately delete the message, but she found herself opening it instead. *Damn her curiosity and competitive spirit.* It would have had to get the better of her eventually. She hadn't responded to the last message from the week prior either where Winter had asked what her vacation plans were this summer. Or the one before that that had come in at two o'clock in the morning with only the words, *I miss you.*

Breakups were never easy, but Summer had had a particularly difficult time deciding to end things with her ex almost two months ago. She and Winter had been together for several years since they had first met at the same college, but their lives couldn't be in more different places now. Winter still lived with her ex-boyfriend—long story for another time—and mostly lived off the royalties from a viral video she'd accidentally done five years ago that was used by a lot of media sites as an ongoing meme and trying to capitalize on those fifteen minutes of fame on her TikTok page. It wasn't a bad life—nor was it particularly wealthy—but it suited Winter just fine. She didn't have much interest or drive in doing more with her life, and that was where things started to strain between them.

Summer couldn't have been more opposite. She had spent every dime she had earned to open up her own business—something she'd been saving for since the age of sixteen when she'd been babysitting neighborhood kids on evenings and weekends for ten dollars an hour. It had all gone to bills and savings, and that meant she'd had a pretty boring college experience compared to some, but it also meant that she was now twenty-five years old and a business owner.

The salon was successful, she might add, too.

Things in the tanning industry never slowed down, and now that it was summer, it was going to be an especially booming season for her. For some reason, people always wanted to prepare for vacation by getting tan instead of getting tan while they were already on vacation.

It seemed like a backwards concept, but she was glad for the business either way.

Even more so because she felt like it was her life's mission to give safe, affordable spray tan options to those who otherwise might have lain out on the beach unprotected or sat under the lights in a tanning bed for an hour. Maybe she was being overcautious, but watching her mother fight melanoma for over two years before losing her battle to skin cancer made Summer more adamant than ever to do what she could to stop it.

She couldn't bring back her mom, but she could damn

well offer safer options to help others never experience what she went through.

That was even part of why she ended things with Winter—which had certainly complicated matters. Winter had been there for her through the acute grief stage, finding her in that low moment and comforting her back to a place where she could finally get out of bed long enough to not cry the moment memories of her mother hit her. Winter had taken her in like a wounded animal, and she seemed to really like that about Summer. Not in a creepy, scary way, but more in a way that just felt like if and when Summer felt the sun again, Winter wasn't going to be interested anymore.

And she wanted to feel the sun. She wanted to pour her grief and sorrow into her business and creating the dream she'd told her mom she would do. So, she walked away from Winter and from the heavy coat of grief feeling like...there must be more.

Being pansexual meant that Summer had dated men, women, and non-binary individuals, but despite her experiences, she'd never yet found someone who felt like they fit. What that meant exactly or what that looked like, she couldn't even explain. All she did know was that she wanted someone who challenged her and pushed her to be the best version of herself—and right now, the only person doing that was herself.

"Summer, do we have an extra potato sack?" Amber, one of the college students who she'd hired part-time for some seasonal work popped her head out from the main supplies closet. "I can't find anything in here that might work to practice with."

She glanced back at her. "We have two in the back room to practice with before tomorrow. Use one of those."

"I can't," Amber said, shaking her head. "I ripped a hole in both of them. These heels just cut right through."

She lifted her foot to show the stiletto heel on the end.

"You tried to practice running in a potato sack in heels?" Summer's brows shot up. *What in the Generation Z was happening right now?*

Amber looked a bit defensive. "There will be people there, Summer. I'm *always* in heels."

Summer was beginning to question her hiring choices, but given the job was to spray naked people, she had a pretty unique set of people applying to work for her. "I'll ask Harold for more. But no more heels in the sack, Amber!"

Amber smirked. "That's what she said."

"Gross." Summer rolled her eyes, but admittedly, she did chuckle slightly at that joke. *That's what she said* jokes never got old—and she'd happily die on that hill to anyone who argued otherwise. "Watch the front desk. I'll be back."

Purse in hand, she headed out into the mall and found herself walking past the raised pavilion where the young man who'd approached her earlier about power for his amp had set up shop. He was singing softly into the microphone, one hand strumming the strings of a guitar as his other hand gripped the neck differently for each varying chord. He didn't seem to notice her, but then again, he didn't seem to notice anyone in that moment.

She paused briefly to watch him—just like a dozen other people were doing as well. He'd actually gained quite the crowd in the short time he'd been singing, and it was no wonder why. His voice was butter—soft, creamy, deep enough to lose yourself in.

Summer glanced down at her arms, seeing small raised bumps breaking out across her skin at the very sound of him. It wasn't even just how he sounded, but there was a weight to everything he was saying. Like his lyrics sat on her heart and weighed her down in all the best ways that love and loss could do.

If she was being fully honest, though, she was also captivated by the way he looked standing on stage. He was tall—a lot taller than her and probably over six feet if she had to guess—but he stood in a way that somehow softened him. Like he was curling into the microphone, caressing it, the way he might hold a woman in his arms...

Why were her thoughts going there?

A flush heated her cheeks. She wasn't about to start fawning over another vendor at the mall right after her own break up. Even if he was tall, dark, and handsome. Good Lord, his jaw line was as hard as the line of his biceps, and his hair was shaved close with a sharp edge and a design crisscrossed through one side of his head. His skin was a deep brown color that jutted against the light brown of the acoustic guitar in his hands. She didn't have the emotional energy to think about his hands or the way they were gripping the neck of the guitar as if he could just snap the entire thing in half with one squeeze.

Nope. Definitely not thinking about those hands.

"Summer!" A young Filipina woman who owned the retro arcade down the corridor pulled Summer from her thoughts. She turned to see that the woman was waving her over.

"Oh, hey Mara," she greeted the woman as she walked away from the singer.

Amara Hart had become a good acquaintance of hers in the last few years since they both owned businesses in the mall. Acquaintances, not friends—but not for the lack of effort on Mara's part. This poor woman invited Summer to everything and even gave her salon shout outs on her Instagram page which had gone viral last year when she'd recorded her engagement story to her now-husband Val, who owned the jewelry store next door. And yet, nine times out of ten, Summer turned down her invitations. Not because she had anything better to do or because she didn't like Mara, but she just…stayed home or worked.

And that was really all she'd been doing for years.

First it had been taking care of her mom while going to school. Then grieving her mom while being with Winter. Now focusing on her business while spending evenings alone with Netflix. When she listed it out like that, it sounded…sad.

She wasn't sad.

But she also wasn't particularly happy. Hell, she had no idea what she was anymore.

Summer walked past a few kiosks selling trinkets, keychains, and candles before she reached the arcade entrance. "How are you, Mara? How's business?"

Mara had one hand on her lower back and the other on her large pregnant belly. Somehow despite her size, she still had on combat boots and a flannel shirt tied around her stomach beneath her baby bump. Until this pregnancy, Summer never would have guessed that Mara was actually a natural dirty blond, but now her roots had grown out pretty far and only the ends of her hair had her colorful purple and pink streaks she'd been so known for.

"I'm about ready to pop out this baby," Mara replied, looking as tired as she sounded. "I swear to gosh, everyone keeps telling me to sleep and rest and all that before the baby gets here, but this third trimester insomnia is next freaking level."

Summer gave her a small smile. "I'm sorry. I can't even

imagine. Is Val helping out a lot at least?"

"He's incredible," Mara confirmed. "The man waits on me hand and foot. He's still cranky that I haven't already gone on maternity leave, but there's no reason I can't do shifts at the arcade until I go into labor."

"I mean, I guess so, but it still sounds like a lot of being on your feet." Summer felt a bit uncomfortable, not knowing what to say in response. She'd never been pregnant and had no experience with kids—or long-term relationships—so this wasn't an area she could relate. Plus, she really just wanted to go finish her errand and get back to work herself. "I'm guessing you guys are going to sit out the Independence Games this year?"

"Absolutely not! I'm not missing an opportunity to put Val in a dunk tank." Mara laughed. "Oh, and did I tell you about Marco?"

Summer shook her head.

"He got accepted into U of M! He's going to college!" Mara was beaming with maternal pride already, though Marco was her foster son until he'd turned eighteen a few months ago.

"That's amazing, Mara. Congratulations! You guys have done amazing work with him." It was definitely something she admired about Mara and the way she gave back to the community. She wasn't a "kid person"—whatever that meant—but she had a lot of respect for those who were. "I'm headed to grab some more potato sacks from the manager's office. Do you need any?"

Mara shook her head. "Val's going to do that one—too risky at my size. I am, however, going to dominate the hot dog eating contest. Someone's going to have to take you down!"

Summer laughed, a grin slipping across her face. Her

winning streak was well known throughout all the mall vendors, but no one had beaten her yet. "Good luck... I hear they raised the jackpot this year, too."

"Five thousand dollars," Mara confirmed. "That's freaking insane for some hot dogs and a water pistol contest, but hey, Harold loves these games almost as much as he loves his Ruth."

"Why do you think he bumped up the prize money this year? I only took home five hundred dollars the last few years when I won." Summer had been contemplating asking Harold about that, but she didn't want to push. She honestly wasn't someone who put her nose in other's business, and she liked to keep her head down for the most part.

But still...it was a large leap in prize winnings.

Mara wiggled her brows conspiratorially. "Rumor has it there's something big coming...like an announcement of some sort."

"Really?" Summer didn't like that at all. Change was not her specialty, and she'd worked hard to get where she was. Having to figure it out again with some new transition wasn't exactly at the top of her list of fun summer plans. "Hmm. Well, if you hear anything, let me know. I'll see you tomorrow!"

"You better come hungry tomorrow!" Mara called out after her.

Summer laughed and turned to wave back at her over her shoulder, but her gaze caught on something—or someone—else entirely. Kamar was standing to the side of the pavilion and staring straight at her, a plastic bottle of water in his hand. He lifted it to his lips and took a long swig—his eyes not leaving her once.

She quickly looked away, swallowing hard as she tried

to tame the flutters happening in her belly. She did not have time for a distraction, and he was *very* distracting.

CHAPTER THREE

KAMAR

THERE WAS no reasonable explanation for why Kamar couldn't keep his gaze off Summer as she talked to a friend in front of the arcade. He tried to tell himself the excuse of that he just needed to take a water break in between sets, but he knew that wasn't true.

The truth was that he found her fascinating.

In the little time he'd known her—all of a few hours—he'd seen someone who was a complete dichotomy in every way. She seemed personable and friendly with the arcade owner, as if they'd known each other for years, and yet the moment she turned and walked away, her face completely fell. Like it had all been an act for the other woman and as soon as she'd been able to drop the facade...she had.

He frowned as he watched her walk away, but tried to push it all away from his mind. He didn't have the time or attention span to focus on this one strange woman who seemed both fulfilled and incredibly sad all at once.

When Kamar glanced back toward the pavilion, he noticed a woman was sitting on the edge of the stage and flipping through his song book.

"Excuse me?" he called out to her as he headed back, putting his hand out for his property. "That's mine."

She glanced up at him, her cheeks flushing a deep red on her olive-tinged skin. "Oh! I'm so sorry!"

He took it from her as she held it out to him. "That's a bit of an odd thing to do, don't you think? Just walk up and look through someone's notebook?"

The woman was standing now, looking like she was ready to run the moment he blinked. "Sorry. I know. That was strange."

Kamar stood there waiting for further explanation, but she just continued to stare at him. A long, awkward moment passed between them. "Uh...well...is there something you needed? Something you were looking for?"

She kept staring. *Good Lord, she wasn't even blinking.*

He was starting to get irritated and waved his hand in front of her face in case she was having some sort of episode. "Hello?"

"Oh, uh...no. Sorry." She was looking around now—her eyes kind of wild. "Just was wondering what made you so...interesting."

Kamar frowned even deeper now. "What?"

"Nothing," the woman quickly replied. "I have to run. It was great to meet you! Happy July Fourth!"

With that, she waved and then waltzed off like they'd just finished a casual, normal conversation.

What in the patriotic bull was that?

Despite his time playing for total strangers over the years, that was definitely one of the strangest experiences he'd had with a groupie. Not that he was popular enough to have a groupie, but he wasn't sure how else to explain that interaction. He glanced through his notebook, filing through the pages to see if anything was altered or missing, but everything looked the same. Hopefully it had just been some sort of innocent curiosity, but he still felt a churn in his gut saying that he'd probably run into her again.

"Hey, Kamar!" Conner, the owner of The Big Cheese Food Truck, walked up to him and put his hand out. They shook and smiled at one another.

Kamar had first met Conner last fall when he'd parked on campus and quickly became the hottest commodity to every college student there. While he wasn't Kamar's favorite person, he did respect that Conner did a lot of work with local underprivileged youth to provide hot breakfasts every morning since the schools did not. "Good to see you, Conner. How's the food truck business?"

"Delicious, as usual," he joked. "But listen, man, I've got a proposition for you."

Kamar lifted one brow. "I'm all ears."

"The Games are starting in two hours," Conner explained. "I'm supposed to be in it along with one of my Cheese Heads and they grated out on me—get it? Grated? Like you do to cheese."

Kamar just stared at the man as if he was insane. Safe bet was that he was.

"So, you in?" Conner asked.

"The games are today?" Kamar hadn't expected the Independence Games to be so soon, but technically...it was the holiday this weekend, so that made some sense. "I don't have a bathing suit."

Conner laughed. "What? That's the whole point of the dunk tank. Dunk you in your clothes. Just take your phone out of your pocket. Anyway, I need a teammate, and one of the Cheese Heads is visiting family this weekend."

"Cheese Head?"

"That's what we call our employees." Conner grinned.

"I'm the Head Cheese and they are the Cheese Heads. Catchy, right?"

Kamar shrugged. "I'm lactose intolerant."

Conner paused for a second, as if absorbing the joke, then laughed so hard that his head tipped backwards. "See, this is exactly why I need you to be my partner. You're a fricking riot, K-dog."

God, he hoped that nickname didn't stick. He mentally reminded himself that Conner was a good guy—just a little annoying. "Uh, sure. Why not? I'm kinda going it alone right now anyway, so might have a better chance at winning with a partner. How does that work? We split up the games?"

The Cheese Head clapped his hands enthusiastically. "Heck yeah! We each do two of the contests and then split the prize money. We're going to dominate that water pistol contest. How's your aim?"

Kamar had never gone hunting or held a gun in his entire life. "I mean, my mom said I finally found my aim around eight or nine years old."

Conner blinked, then burst out laughing once more. *Jeez, this guy was easily amused.* "You are a trip, K-dog. An absolute trip. I'll see you at the contest."

He shook his hand and then went back up onto the pavilion to start his next set. Kamar played five songs straight through. When he checked his Venmo app, he'd already made over one hundred dollars in tips by the time he had to head out to the contest. Pretty decent for an afternoon, though he hoped to improve that number this weekend when people were watching the fireworks.

What was better than a soundtrack during a firework show? That would be the real money maker.

"Over here!" Conner waved Kamar over as he walked

up to the site where the games would be held. He'd finished his set, packed up his gear and equipment, and locked it up safely in the manager's office before making his way out to where the games would be held. "K-dog! Over here!"

The mall was shaped like a circle and in the center was a large, open-air courtyard with benches and picnic tables where people would congregate after they grabbed something to eat from the food court. Today was a different story, however, because the entire thing was cleared out and there was a full-on stadium set up instead.

Metal bleachers had been erected to one side of the courtyard—already partially filled with people, some of whom he recognized as vendors from different parts of the mall and some who he had never seen before. Not too far to the left of the bleachers was a bright blue dunk tank and a woman with streaked purple hair in a braid down her back was standing in front of it—hands on her hips. She was standing by the owner of the bar, The Lucky Leprechaun, and talking animatedly as if gearing up for the competition.

He had a feeling people were going to be taking today pretty seriously.

"It's Kamar," he reminded Conner as he reached him. "Not really the nickname type."

Conner's face flushed for only a quick moment before he shook it off. "Cool. I respect that. Listen, there are two rounds—first round is getting the water aimed at that pedal to make the deer race. The second round is how many deer can you knock over with the water pistol. Which one do you want to do?"

"The race," he said immediately, even though the entire thing seemed like an odd pastime. "I'm not really the hunting type."

"You should have seen the deer I bagged last year,"

Conner launched into a story that Kamar had zero interest in hearing. He nodded along, dropping in a few "huhs" and an "is that so?" or two. But his attention had been pulled away almost immediately when he saw Summer walking into the courtyard.

She had black streaks across both of her cheeks like she was ready for battle. They were in sharp contrast with her pale skin and the red, white, and blue bandana she had pulled over her hair. Her normally thick, curly mane was tied back underneath it, sticking out the back in a ponytail instead.

Kamar lifted his hand to wave at her, but she didn't see him. Her eyes were focused on the deer race game, which was set up on the far wall across from the bleachers. She walked around the perimeter, seeming to survey the entire game from all angles.

He couldn't help but chuckle. *This chick is really trying to win.*

"Oh, some of my cheese heads are here! Can't believe they showed up after telling me they couldn't make it." Conner pointed up at the bleachers to two teenagers wearing literal cheese hats. *Is that their uniform?* "I'm going to go say hi in a passive aggressive way before the games start."

Kamar didn't follow him, instead turning his gaze back to Summer.

"Hey." He pulled at her attention as he walked up to her as casually as he could. *Was he strutting?* God, he hoped he wasn't strutting. "You look ready for some competition."

She eyed him for a moment, before returning her gaze to the game. "There's face paint by the west entrance if you want some."

Suddenly a loud shouting sound came from over by the

bleachers, and they both turned to look for the source. The two cheese heads at the top of the bleacher were shouting down toward the ground, crossing their arms over their head as if they were trying to stop someone...or something.

Kamar lowered his gaze to where they were looking and spotted...*cheese everywhere.*

Like, an actual melted stream of cheese was shooting up into the air over the bleachers in a shockingly high arc for what seemed like a pretty thick queso. Conner was standing on the ground by the end of the bleachers holding what could only be described as a muenster of a cheese cannon pointed directly north.

As the cheese reached a peak several feet above him, it turned directions and rained gouda all over Conner's head, shoulders, and upper torso.

"It's hot!" Conner shouted, dropping the cannon to the ground and hopping around on one foot and then the other, as if he could just shake the melted cheddar from his skin. Spoiler alert: It wasn't going anywhere. "Get it off me!"

The attendant from the dunk tank ran over to him with towels and began wiping him down as he squirmed and thrashed around.

"What the heck just happened?" Summer asked.

Kamar's eyes were wide, and he shook his head. "I'm not sure I have the words to properly describe what I just witnessed."

She laughed and leaned toward him, this time placing her hand on his shoulder. Was she softening to him? This was the most at ease he'd seen her so far, and he'd be lying if he didn't admit that the skin on his shoulder where she was touching felt like it was on fire.

"I don't think I do either," she admitted, still leaning into him.

Please don't let go.

"I hope he's okay...you don't think it burned him, do you?"

Kamar shook his head. "I think he'd have passed out from the pain by now if it was that hot. Or he'd be screaming more. He seems more like he's thoroughly inconvenienced and pissed as hell about it."

They watched for another moment as Conner finished toweling off—a huge scowl on his face as his orangey-yellow stained clothes were already beginning to smell under the summer sun. He was now arguing with his cheese heads who they could hear apologizing for breaking the cheese cannon and not warning him earlier before he detonated it all over himself.

Who the heck has a cheese cannon anyway?

"Guess that means he's not going to be competing in the first race," Summer mused, her hand falling from Kamar's shoulder as she looked back.

"Crap," he muttered, mostly under his breath, but she'd heard him anyway.

Summer frowned. "What's wrong?"

"He was my partner." Kamar scratched at the stubble on his chin that had been growing longer throughout the day. He hadn't really been looking forward to this as a solo expedition, but it seemed there were other vendors here doing it alone as well.

She seemed to study him for a moment, biting the bottom edge of her lip as she pulled it in between her teeth and then let it go. "I guess I could...I mean...if you want to partner with me, I guess that would be fine."

Now it was his turn to study her expression—and conflicted didn't even begin to describe it. "Aren't you like a four-time winner at this point? And suddenly you want to split the grand prize?"

"I do *not* want to split anything," she clarified, lifting one finger up between them. "But...I mean, I'm probably not winning any favors with all the vendors if I were to win again by myself. As part of a team, maybe it won't seem so greedy."

Kamar laughed and shook his head. "Gee, how heroic and altruistic of you to include me."

Her cheeks tinged a shade of pink before she shrugged her shoulders and smiled. "If I was a man, you would probably be calling me smart. Competitiveness isn't considered a character flaw if you have a penis."

"Touché," he agreed, a little disappointed with himself that he hadn't considered it from that angle. "Sorry about that. In that case...no, thank you."

She frowned. "What?"

"I don't want to be your teammate," Kamar continued. "I'm going to play solo. So are you. May the best person win."

Her lips twitched slightly at the corners, and she tipped up her chin. Finally, she smiled and nodded in agreement. "Game on."

CHAPTER FOUR

SUMMER

"You CAN CATCH up in the sack race," Mara assured Summer as they huddled together at the starting line of the Potato Sack Race. "That water pistol game is rigged, I swear."

In the deer-shooting water pistol game, she'd come in second place to Kamar—which was absolutely *not* going to happen again. How the heck it had even happened the first time was mind boggling to her, but damn if she didn't respect his aim.

After she'd asked him to partner with her and he'd said no, she'd felt a bit of her guard between him and her coming down. He wasn't someone to just follow the lead because she said so, a quality she really admired in...well, anyone. She knew her personality tended to be the Type A strong-headed one, and that meant it was really easy to bulldoze others and not think about their feelings.

She was working on that in weekly therapy, because, after Winter, vulnerability wasn't her strong suit. Which made it all the more strange that she was allowing Mara to be her cheerleader in this moment.

It was almost like she was beginning to let people in again—kidding. That was definitely not going to happen.

"Do you think I should try hopping two feet together, or one and then the other?" Summer asked Mara as she studied the course in front of them and tried to push away any thoughts of the man standing a few sacks to her right.

It was a straight shot to the finish line, and everyone else was lined up next to her stepping into their potato sacks ready for the short sprint. She could probably get there in thirty seconds, but she'd have to start strong and then keep the lead.

"I'd keep your feet together," Mara said, her fingers curled under her chin as she contemplated the course. "Long hops with tons of power—really push off the ground."

Summer nodded. "Makes sense."

"You've got this!" Mara patted her on the back once and then stepped away. She'd been in the first round of games but hadn't gotten a high enough score to qualify for the next. She and about half of the other mall vendors were now in the bleachers or on the sidelines watching everyone else compete to see if they'd make it to the hot dog eating contest next.

Harold stepped to the finish line and blew on a small whistle that was hanging around his neck. "On the count of three!"

Everyone quickly finished getting in their sacks and poised at the starting line.

Harold lifted a red flag on a wooden stick above his head. "One! Two!"

He paused, and the lady who owned Pane in the Glass Window Repair fell forward, having gotten a false start.

"Three! Go!" Harold waved the flag down in one long

arc and everyone took off—expect the window repair lady who was now tangled in her sack and trying to get out.

Summer pushed off the ground with every bit of power in her and kept her eyes on the finish line. She heard panting and puffing and shouting from everyone racing around her, but she kept her focus on one thing and one thing only—winning.

Finally, she was close enough for one last push and Summer threw her entire body forward, arms outstretched wide as she landed just a few centimeters over the finish line.

"And we have a winner!" Harold was now standing next to her and waving the flag wildly around over his head. He reached for her hand and grabbed it, lifting it up in the air. "*Summer's Sun* is our second-round winner!"

"Go, Summer!" A voice called out.

She turned to see Kamar just crossing the finish line, dropping his potato sack, and clapping for her. Her cheeks felt hot, and she grinned at the other contestants—most of whom seemed happy for her. The hair stylist who owned Barber Streisand was the only one who seemed to be sporting a pout, but Summer tried not to pay attention to the haters.

One of the things she and her mom had bonded over was the love of competition. There wasn't anything that the two of them hadn't turned into a contest. Who can cook breakfast the fastest? Who can collect the most pinecones outside to make a centerpiece for Thanksgiving? Who is the safer driver—that one came with a little device in both of their cars from the car insurance company that kept track of every move they made. Summer would win occasionally, but her mom never played easy on her.

It wasn't cutthroat, though. No bad blood or sore losers.

But after her mother died, competitions didn't have the same energy or enjoyment they'd once had for Summer. In her period of grief, she gave up any sort of drive and just let Winter take care of her. It wasn't who she really was, or who she wanted to be. Her mother had loved the competitive, driven side of her. And she wanted that back. She wanted that feeling she'd get when she'd smile at her mom and they'd high-five over some win.

Hell, she really just wanted her mom back.

But that wasn't an option, so she had decided to start winning instead. And now? Well, now it was a bit hard to *not* be cutthroat. Losing felt...personal. Emotional. She took it hard, and so she pushed herself even harder. Every race, contest, and competition were for her mother...

Even the Yule Heights Independence Games.

She made a mental note to herself that she should probably bring that up in therapy at some point.

"You launched yourself across that course, I swear," Kamar praised as he approached her.

Everyone was beginning to head toward the third race—the hotdog eating contest. To the far end of the courtyard were several long tables lined up in a row that had dozens—maybe hundreds—of fully cooked hotdogs in hotdog buns stacked on a plate in front of each person's station.

"This, though," Kamar continued, now pointing to the table full of hotdogs. "This is where I'll shine. You cannot fit more hot dogs in your mouth than I can."

Summer smirked at him, glancing sideways as they walked side by side. "You're an expert at swallowing a long sausage, huh?"

His cheeks darkened and he snorted a laugh. "Okay, okay. I walked right into that one."

"I wouldn't underestimate me in this challenge either,"

Summer joked, then placed her hand on her stomach, giving it a light pat. "I skipped lunch just to prepare for this. I've got the room."

Kamar turned his head to look at her, his gaze starting low at her feet then sliding up her body until he met her eyes. *Holy hell.* She felt like her skin was set on fire just from the way he looked at her, and her breath caught in her throat.

"I'd like to see that," he said in response.

Summer cleared her throat and looked away, but when she did, her thoughts were interrupted by a familiar sight. "Winter?"

"Team Summer!" Her ex-girlfriend was standing by the table of hotdogs wearing an olive-green shirt that had a bright yellow illustrated sun design on the front. She had two small American flags in each hand and was waving them around like her own personal cheerleader. "Hip-hip-hooray!"

"Is she a friend of yours?" Kamar asked, his brows furrowing. He looked almost upset to see her, which was kind of odd since he didn't know Winter at all.

Summer shook her head. "Uh, not really. More like my ex-girlfriend."

"Your ex?" His eyes widened slightly as he turned back to her. "Oh. Ohhhh. So..."

"I'm pansexual," she clarified quickly, already knowing where that question was going.

It used to really bother her that she had to clarify her sexuality for every new person she met—since when do straight people have to do that? But, over the years, she'd kind of accepted that people were curious, and that wasn't always a bad thing. In fact, sometimes it was a great opener into acceptance or allowing a safe place for others to feel that they could be honest about who they were as well.

"Do you like it?" Winter asked as she turned away from Summer and pointed to the back of her shirt which said in all capital letters TEAM SUMMER. "I'm your one-woman cheer squad!"

"I'm also cheering her on," Kamar added to the conversation as he stepped up next to her. "Nice to see you again."

Summer frowned. *See you again?* "What?"

"Aren't you also in the race?" Winter asked Kamar, her hands now on her hips.

She wasn't exactly glaring, but Summer could see frustration in Winter's expression. *Do they know one another?*

"One of us is going to get knocked out in this round, so if it's me, I can cheer her on in the last round." Kamar shrugged, seemingly unfazed by her question or guarded stance.

Harold blew the whistle indicating that the hot-dog eating contest was about to start.

"Uh...we should probably get to our stations," Summer said. "But, uh...I guess thanks for coming, Winter."

She made a second mental note to add *boundary issues* to her next therapy meeting topic list.

"Anything for my girl," Winter replied, leaning in and placing a kiss on her cheek. She squeezed Summer's hand before she pushed away, turned her eyes on Kamar, and gave him an assured smirk.

Gosh, she did not miss Winter's jealous streak.

"Players, get your bibs on and get ready!" Harold gave instructions to everyone as they sat in front of their plates piled high with plain hotdogs tucked into buns.

Summer hurried to her seat and quickly fastened the plastic bib around her neck and rubbed some hand sanitizer on her hands. If she was about to wreak havoc on a plate of dogs, she might as well clean up first.

"Ready?" Kamar asked, his voice lowered as he spoke over Harold's instructions from where he was sitting next to her.

She propped up her arms on the side of the table, adjusting her elbows to give herself more room as she stretched her neck from side to side. *It's time to get down to business.* "Absolutely."

"Ready! Set!" Harold began, raising his flag high in the air above his head.

Everyone at the table was poised and staring at him. Summer could hear Winter cheering from the sidelines, but she didn't turn to look at her.

"And...GO!" Harold waved the flag down in one long sweeping manner.

Hotdogs slammed into face holes at record speed.

Summer was swallowing her third when she felt her stomach lurch. She put a hand to her mouth, trying to convince the contents to stay down.

"You got this, Summer!" Winter shouted from somewhere in her peripheral.

Kamar nudged her arm with his elbow, and she glanced at him just long enough to see two hotdogs sticking out of his mouth side-by-side. He had also crossed his eyes.

She nearly choked on the hotdog as it went down.

"Cheater!" she gasped, laughing as she finally swallowed it. "Don't make me laugh!"

He grinned, already shoving the next hotdog into his mouth.

She turned her focus back on her own plate and the next few went down without an issue. Everyone had been provided a glass of water and Summer dunked her hotdogs and buns in the water before eating them in order to make the bread less voluminous. They went down a lot quicker that way, but they tasted horrible.

Like, beyond horrible.

Watery bread dogs were certainly not going to be the highlight of her day.

"Is he okay?" Harold's voice was somehow reaching her over the sound of dozens of slurped meat dogs.

Summer knew she should just focus on her plate, but curiosity got the better of her and she glanced up anyway to look. Harold was squinting his eyes and pointing next to her. She turned to see Kamar had gotten very still—he wasn't grabbing at the hotdogs. Instead, he was grabbing at his throat and trying to bang a fist against his chest.

No sound was coming out at all.

Without a second thought, Summer jumped up out of her chair and got behind him. She pulled him up out of his chair as he scrambled to get to his feet with her. His eyes were wide and the look of fear on his face only spurred her to move faster. Standing behind him, her chest to his back, Summer wrapped her arms around his waist and began performing the Heimlich maneuver.

One push. Two. Three pushes in and up.

Kamar coughed, leaning forward as he finally began gasping for air.

"Are you okay?" she asked, letting go and coming around him to check his airway. He was definitely breathing now—the hotdog he must have been choking on was clearly dislodged.

Suddenly a loud bell rang, and Summer realized that this round was over.

Kamar looked at her with wild eyes, but his focus was on her plate instead of himself. "Did you win?"

She still had six hotdogs left on her plate and she'd origi-nally had fifteen.

Nine hot dogs. Three less than last year.

Harold came over and checked on Kamar to make sure he was okay. Kamar confirmed that he was as Summer stepped back over to her plate and counted the remaining hotdogs one more time. There was no way she would win with only nine in one minute, but honestly...it didn't matter.

She felt okay. Like, more than okay.

There wasn't a shadow of a doubt in her mind that she'd made the right choice to help Kamar, and honestly, she still felt kind of proud that she'd eaten nine hotdogs and saved a man's life in less than a minute.

If there was a competition for that, clearly she'd crush it.

"Summer, I'm so sorry." Kamar put a hand on her arm after Harold had walked away. "I cost you the round."

"Not necessarily," she assured him, shaking her head and pointing to the tray. "I ate nine. How many did you eat?"

Kamar counted the ones still left on his plate and then grinned sheepishly at her. "Five...and a half if you count the one I choked on."

Summer laughed. "You cannot count that one. I'm just glad you're okay."

He smiled a bit wider at that statement and ducked his head. "I can't say I've ever choked on a sausage in front of a woman I like before."

A woman I like. Her breath was stuck in her lungs for a moment too long, and she had to clear her throat before she could focus on him. Finally, she smiled and shrugged her shoulders as if she was completely nonchalant. "There's always a first time for everything."

"And Summer Darby is our third-round winner!" Harold announced over the megaphone.

She looked up to see him walking over to her with a shiny golden hotdog on a ribbon.

Harold lifted it over her head and let it hang around her neck. "Congratulations, darling. You're looking like a ringer again this year."

"Thanks," she said, trying not to let her eyes find Kamar even though she could feel him watching her. He liked her...what did that mean? Like, romantically? She certainly found him attractive—anyone with eyes would. The way he commanded a stage was effortless and women were lining up to listen to the soft way he sung ballads. But was she even ready to date again?

"You're like an actual hero," Winter interrupted her thoughts as she threw her arms around Summer's neck.

Even if she was ready to date again, it seemed like Winter was not ready to let her go.

CHAPTER FIVE

KAMAR

"You alive enough to be dunked?" Harold asked Kamar as the crowd moved from the hot dog eating contest toward the area with the dunk tank. "I mean, now that you're out of the running, we could use some dunking volunteers."

"I think I could manage that," Kamar agreed, patting his hand to his chest. "I'm all good."

"Don't feel bad, you know. I've been doing this contest for years, and someone usually chokes," Harold admitted. "Ruth told me not to do it again this year—too much of a liability. But, what can I say? I'm a traditional man. Wouldn't be fair to have the last Independence Games without it, you know?"

"The last?" Kamar's brows lifted.

Harold nodded, but then put a finger to his lips and lowered his voice. "It's not exactly widespread news yet, but Yule Heights Shopping Center was purchased by a new owner. They're bringing in their own team to run and manage everything, so I'm officially headed into retirement."

Kamar frowned. "Oh, man. I'm sorry, Harold."

"Don't be!" He shook his head. "I've been waiting on this day a long time. Plus, you should see the retirement package they set up for me. I'll be just fine. Ruth and I already have our first vacation planned for the fall."

He smiled at the older man, a warmth in his chest as he thought of his parents yet again. "Where are you guys going?"

"Cawker City, Kansas," Harold replied. "You ever seen the world's largest ball of twine? Mr. Jaziri, you have not lived until you've put your eyes on that beauty."

Kamar didn't have a response for that one, but just smiled and patted Harold on the back. "Always a pleasure talking to you, Harold."

The older man grinned back at him, then lifted the megaphone to his mouth and began shouting directions for the dunk tank contest. The participants who hadn't scored in the top three places in the last contest were now the dunkees—including Kamar.

He took off his sneakers and tucked his phone into them, putting them out of way of the dunk tanks so that they wouldn't get wet.

"You should get in the third tank," Summer said, pointing toward one of the dunk tanks. "That's the one I'll be hitting."

He lifted his brows and smirked. "And you want to dunk me?"

"I mean, it's only fair. I did save your life, so the least you can let me do is potentially threaten it again."

Kamar laughed. "You know, Harold said basically the same thing. My rep is not doing too well here today, huh."

Summer shrugged. "I wouldn't say that."

He sensed there was something more she wanted to say. "I'm glad to know I still have someone's interest peaked."

The woman he'd first seen stealing a peek through his notebook joined them, her arm around Summer's waist. "You're going to win again, Summer. For sure."

"Thanks, Winter." Her eyes darted awkwardly between the woman and Kamar. "Uh, can I talk to you privately for a minute?"

"Always." The woman walked off with Summer a little way.

Why had Summer's ex-girlfriend been looking through his notebook? He still couldn't piece it all together. The woman just seemed all around kind of bizarre.

Kamar climbed into the dunk tank that she had originally pointed to, waving at the other two dunkees in the nearby tanks. He recognized the female bar owner of The Lucky Leprechaun, Saoirse, in the tank next to him but wasn't sure who the man was in the last one.

"Good luck!" Saoirse gave him a thumbs up.

He did the same back to her, then found Summer again. Her conversation with Winter was looking heated and finally Winter walked off and left the courtyard completely. Kamar wanted to ask what was going on between them, but this was new territory for him. He liked Summer, and he'd made that pretty clear from the beginning.

But he'd never competed with another woman...for a woman.

Heck, for all he knew, he was completely reading the signs wrong. Summer might not even be interested in him. Wait...what was he even talking about?

He was not interested in dating anyone right now. School. Work. Those were where his focus needed to be. And yet, he couldn't seem to help himself when he watched

Summer walk back across the courtyard and stand at the throwing line in front of his dunk tank.

She was beautiful—no doubt there. But there was more to it than that. She was intriguing and enigmatic, and there was something ferocious about her that he wanted to see more of.

"You ready?" Summer called out, breaking his concentration. She tossed a baseball up in the air and then caught it in her other hand.

He gave her a thumbs up, then held the edges of the seat he was sitting on.

"But we have a twist!" Harold announced to the crowd. "This isn't just a normal dunk tank contest…"

Harold, please don't.

"You all know the rules—you each get three balls to rotate through and whoever knocks their opponent in first is the winner. But we added something a little extra special this year." Harold wiggled his brows and clearly loved that he had a secret. "Conner, arm our dunkees!"

Conner came walking out with a large bin and an even larger smile. His shirt was still stained with cheese from the earlier cheese cannon disaster and his hair was slicked back and wet. He stopped at each dunk tank and pulled out a large super soaker water gun and handed it to each person who was about to be dunked. The one he handed Kamar was neon green with stripes of orange down the side.

"In this dunk tank contest, the dunkees get the chance to defend themselves!" Harold continued. "As you're trying to hit the buzzer and knock them down, they're allowed to try to hit you with their water guns and knock you off course!"

Kamar tested his water gun, shooting it straight north.

The stream went incredibly high, and he shot Summer a devilish grin. "Oh, this is going to be fun."

She looked unconcerned. "I can still hit the target just fine!"

"Challenge accepted," he called back.

Harold began his countdown and then sounded a buzzer to begin the race.

The ball was already leaving Summer's hand the moment it started, but she was about an inch too far to the left to make contact with the target. Kamar lifted his water gun and began shooting it at her, aiming it a bit higher than her head so that it would arc down and land on her since she was so far away.

She gasped as the cold water made contact. "Hey!"

Now she was swinging harder, rotating through balls quickly as she tried to see clearly to hit the target, but he kept blocking her view. Kamar's view, however, was mercifully unblocked. And by that, he meant Summer's very wet, very clingy T-shirt. He found his eyes wandering more than a few times but kept trying to refocus himself.

Suddenly she grinned, and he realized that she'd just caught him staring at her chest. His hand pulled off the trigger for a second too long and she leaned forward even farther, her arms pushing in on either side of her chest. *Was she doing that on purpose?*

When his eyes met hers and he saw the determination on her face, he realized that she was. He also realized—a moment too late—that she'd just thrown a ball and the clang he heard was that ball making contact with the dunk tank target.

The seat beneath him gave way and he dropped the water gun as he was plunged into what might have been the coldest bath of his entire freaking life. If someone had told him that they had imported this water directly from the North Pole, he would have believed them.

"Ah!" Kamar shouted as he came up to the surface and shook the water from his hair and wiped at his face. "Why's it so dang cold?"

"I won!" Summer threw her hands up in the air and was jumping up and down.

"And we have a winner!" Harold walked over to her with a large trophy—seriously, it was probably about half his height—and handed it to her.

Conner handed Kamar a towel and gave him a hand as he stepped out of the dunk tank. "Man, you sunk like a stone."

Kamar laughed and wiped himself dry. "Thanks, man. Always great to meet a fan."

That made the Head Cheese laugh and he patted him on the back. "Free grilled cheese on me later, man. Just stop by the truck. Great job today!"

"Thanks," Kamar replied as he headed more his shoes and phone. With the number of hot dogs he'd consumed, a sandwich did not sound very appealing at the moment.

Once he was as dry as he was going to get, he put his shoes back on and checked the messages on his phone. His dad had checked in on him, and he sent a quick response back to tell him how the day was going.

"I couldn't have done it without you, you know," Summer said as she sidled up to him a few minutes later. She had the large golden trophy in her arms, and it took him a moment to realize that the figurine on the top was, in fact, a large hot dog. "I should really split this thing with you, but it'll look so great in the middle of my small apartment's living room."

He nearly snorted his laugh. "I don't know much about

interior design, but clearly every good living space needs this perfect aesthetic addition. Harold clearly has an eye on him."

"Hey, do you...uh, would you be interested in grabbing a drink?" Summer put the trophy down on the ground in front of her and seemed to be purposely avoiding any eye contact. "There's this great bar here—the Irish pub. They're giving out shots to all the contestants before the fireworks later."

Kamar patted his stomach, trying to gauge how well those hotdogs from earlier were sitting. "I could maybe fit one shot in on top of all those dogs."

She grinned, and then a look of nausea passed over her face, too. "Yeah, I know what you mean. My stomach is pretty mad at me right now."

"Nothing a glass of alcohol can't fix," he teased, because he didn't want to think about his schoolwork right now. He didn't want to think about the set he'd need to be playing later. He didn't want to think about anything other than being around this woman for a few more minutes.

CHAPTER SIX

I ASKED HIM OUT. Summer ruminated on the thought as she and Kamar walked all the way back toward her store and his music stand. *I can't believe I asked him out on a date.* Though the more she thought about it, the more she wasn't convinced she had. Technically, she'd invited him to join all the other contestants.

Did he know it was a date? Did she want it to be a date?

This was exactly why she avoided all of this. New starts were so dang complicated. Everything was up in the air, and she had no idea where she stood with this man she'd just met. Heck, she didn't even know where she wanted to stand with him. God, he was so cute though.

"Let me just run into the store and drop off my stuff really quick," she told him, then pointed toward the entrance to the bar. "I'll meet you there?"

Kamar nodded and headed in that direction.

Summer headed straight to the small bathroom by her office and quickly reapplied some lipstick, fluffed her hair up a bit where the super soaker had watered it down, and then put on a fresh, dry shirt that didn't have ketchup stains.

She was primping. Good lord, she was someone who primped now.

"Over here," Kamar called out to her with a wave as she walked into the bar a few minutes later.

Saoirse and her wife were standing at the bar and filling up about thirty different shot glasses with a bright yellow liquid. She waved at them and then saw Mara standing by Kamar.

"Oh my gosh, that is perfect," Mara was saying as Summer walked up to the duo. "Do you sell on Spotify? Or where?"

Kamar nodded. "Yeah, but I have some CD's if you want to go old school."

Mara turned to Summer and grabbed her arm, then rubbed her own pregnant belly. "Guess what! He's got his own demo and it's all soft ballads. How perfect, right?"

"For...?" Summer wasn't sure she was following.

"Summer! For my birthing soundtrack, obviously," Mara clarified. "I need to be listening to something love-filled and soothing when I bring this little kiddo into the world, and what could be better than *Music Like the Moon?* It's almost too perfect, it's that dreamy."

Summer laughed; her brows raised. "Is that when you know you've hit the big times, Kamar?"

"When someone gives birth to my song?" Kamar nodded his head as he chuckled. "Yeah, I'd say that is definitely a qualifier for the Billboard Top 100."

"Drop it by the arcade before you leave tonight," Mara said. "I have to go pee. This child is dancing on my bladder. Bye!"

With that, the small woman ran off and Summer was left with a warmth in her chest that she recognized as...

affection? Was she becoming friends with these people? Or even more preposterous—were they already friends?

All she could hear in her gut was—*I hope so.*

Kamar handed her a shot glass from the bar, picking one up for himself as well. "Cheers to your big win."

She smiled, wanting to really enjoy the moment for herself too. Sometimes life got so busy that she was always focused on the next competition and not reveling in her current win. Today, she just wanted to be present. She wanted to be here...with him.

They clinked glasses and then both swallowed their shots. Her stomach churned at the liquid fighting the hotdogs, but the drink cleared her throat anyway.

"Thank you. I am surprised I won, to be honest." Summer cleared her throat, but then accidentally let out a burp that reveled the decibel levels of a foghorn. "Oh my gosh, I'm so sorry."

Kamar tipped his head back and laughed. "Wow. That was actually pretty impressive."

"You didn't hear that!" Heat flooded her cheeks, and she put a hand to her forehead dramatically. "I can't believe I did that on a date."

"Date?" Kamar's brows lifted so high they almost ran into his hairline. "This is a date?"

Please, just let me go die right now.

"Um..." Summer found herself at a loss for words. "I mean, if you...it could be, sort of. Um, you know..."

Kamar grinned, and his dark eyes seemed illuminated with joy. "I'm in."

"You are?" She wasn't sure why she was so nervous right now, but suddenly she was very aware of how she was standing and the way her arm was propped up on the bar.

"I'm sorry if that's weird. I thought we were...I don't know... feeling a vibe?"

"I absolutely was feeling that, too," he agreed, now leaning in a little closer. "Or I was until your ex-girlfriend staked her claim. Wasn't sure if that meant you were available or not."

"Oh, Winter?" Summer shook her head. "No, that ended a while ago."

"Your ex is named Winter?" Kamar was smiling wide again. "And you're Summer? Yeah, crazy how those two didn't work out."

She playfully shoved his upper arm. "I mean, you'd think I'd have seen the signs earlier."

"The heart wants what the heart wants," Kamar agreed, then turned to order two more shots from the bartender. "You up for one more?"

"Just one," she confirmed, lifting a solitary finger. "But maybe I'll have some water first."

"Good idea," he agreed, adding two glasses of water to the order. "Speaking of the heart..."

She raised her brows, already anticipating his next question.

"Well, I mean, Winter and I don't exactly fit in the same category," Kamar continued, his voice soft and nonjudgmental. "Like, any of them at all."

Summer laughed at that comparison. "That's very fair."

"So, what does your heart want?"

She shrugged as she accepted the glass of water the bartender placed in front of her. "I don't think my heart puts people into categories, you know? It just follows what it feels. Sometimes that's a woman, sometimes that's a man. It all depends on the heart inside, you know?"

He nodded thoughtfully. "I like that. Admittedly, I'm a little intimidated by it as well."

"Intimidated?" Summer frowned now.

He looked away for a moment, then back at her. "That probably sounds ridiculous, but I'm just being honest. I've never dated anyone who doesn't identify as completely straight before."

"Are you not open to that?" she asked, now feeling almost a bit defensive. Living in the current day and time and area she lived in, she didn't have to often defend her sexuality to people, but it still did happen on occasion.

"I'm absolutely open to that," Kamar responded almost immediately. He placed his hand on her upper arm that was resting on the bar. "I'm sorry. I didn't mean anything by that, other than this would be a new experience for me. One that I'm more than open to. Love is love, right?"

She smiled a bit more cautiously this time. "Well, what about you? You know all this information about me—where I work, who I date—and I know next to nothing about you."

"Ask away," he replied, his hands up in the air like he was an open book. "It's not a very glamorous life, but I'm finishing my Master's degree in music education at U of M, doing gigs on the side to support myself. I'm originally from New York. My father stayed out there when I came here for school since my mother died several years ago. He's a great man, but he's stubborn. After my mother died, he just kind of decided that was all he wanted out of life. Refuses to try anything new, even though I asked him to move here with me. I still try and get back and visit him at least once a month."

"I'm so sorry." It was Summer's turn to reach out now, her hand lightly on his knee. "About your mom. That's... well, I'm pretty familiar with that loss unfortunately."

"Skin cancer?" Kamar asked.

She was surprised he'd put together the pieces of that puzzle. "Is it that obvious?"

"You mentioned at the store earlier that healthy tanning options were a cause important to your heart...so, it just made sense." Kamar shrugged. "Your mom?"

Summer nodded. "Yeah, she was both mom and dad to me my entire life. She was a powerhouse."

"I know the type," he replied, and something about the depth of his tone told her he really did.

They were both quiet for a moment, just looking at one another. His gaze was soft, though, and she felt like she and her story were being held without any words or any hands. He was just sitting with her in the grief of losing her mother, and not trying to do anything about it. In previous relationships, when she'd shared about her history or upbringing, the person went into fix-it mode and tried to make her feel better. Hell, that's all Winter had done—comfort her and try to make her feel better. He wasn't doing that at all, and it was refreshing.

She didn't need to feel better. She liked her life exactly as it was, and she wanted to sit in the sadness for the parts that were sad. It felt genuine and important to not sugarcoat her life with a highlight reel, but to honor it with every scar and tumble she'd taken along the way.

"If she created you," Kamar replied, "I can imagine she was formidable."

Summer smiled and looked down at her hand still on his knee. "I could say the same thing about your mom."

"Abso-freaking-lutely," he agreed, then grabbed the shot glasses off the bar and handed one to her. "To our moms."

She took one from him and clinked the edge of her glass against his. "To moms."

CHAPTER SEVEN

KAMAR

"You're going viral, man." Conner held up his cell phone to Kamar, the screen illuminated with a TikTok video set to Jaws-themed music.

Kamar felt a flicker of excitement—had someone recorded one of his performances? He took the phone from Conner, looking closer at the video. Definitely not a performance. *What the hell?* It was footage of him falling into the dunk tank during the Independence Games, but then someone had added an animated shark to the water that was then pretending to attack and eat him.

The dunk tank turned red with animated blood and then the screen went black except for the words: R.I.P. TO THE MAN WHO STOLE MY GIRL.

"What the hell?" Kamar frowned and looked up at Conner. "This is...this is creepy. Is this a threat or something?"

Conner shrugged. "It was posted by someone named @winteriscoming69 last night and already has over fifty thousand views. People think the animation work is funny and the topic relatable, apparently. They're calling it a Skeet-video rip off, like Kanye did against his ex-wife's new man. The top comment just says 'Rest in Pieces.' The one under that is 'Savage!' Who did you piss off, guy?"

He knew the answer to that immediately, even though it still didn't make any sense.

"Are you headed to the fireworks?" Kamar asked Conner instead.

Conner shook his head. "I've got to be up early tomorrow. You have fun though! I saw you hobnobbing it with Summer. You should definitely make your move. She's a wonderful girl!"

"You never made your move?" he asked, one brow raised.

Conner laughed. "She's got too many boobs and not enough dick to be my type."

Kamar laughed, because he could kind of see that now that Conner had outed himself. "Okay, okay. I read you loud and clear."

"But, hey, if you are working tomorrow, stop by and grab a cheese sammy on me!" Conner headed off down the mall corridor, leaving Kamar sitting on the bench in front of Lord of the Rinse Dry Cleaners.

"You ready?"

He turned to see Summer walking up to him, and she was holding out a large churro wrapped in parchment paper.

She smiled. "I grabbed us some churros for the show."

"That looks delicious," he replied, taking one from her and chomping off one large bite. After their conversation last night in the bar, he'd asked her to watch the fireworks with him tonight. The mall parking lot was the best vantage point to view them, and so he had seen that people were beginning to camp out a spot in the early afternoon. He hoped they'd still be able to find a good spot, even though they'd waited until the end of the shift. "Hey, uh...I feel like I should tell you something."

Summer's brow furrowed as she looked sideways at him, her churro half sticking out of her mouth. "Uh oh."

"It's not bad," he assured her, but then paused. "Well, I mean...I don't know what it is. It's just weird. Here, let me show you."

He pulled up the video on his phone that Conner had texted him and turned the screen toward Summer. She was quiet for a moment as she watched the screen, then her eyes went wide and found his.

"What the hell? Who posted that?" She took his phone from him and clicked on the profile. "Oh my gosh, Winter!"

"She's, uh, not really taking this breakup too well, is she?" Kamar tried to laugh a little at that, but he was a little skeeved out himself by the entire thing. He'd never been the center of attention unless he was on stage, and so to have that in his personal life felt...uncomfortable, at best.

Summer handed his phone back to him, her face downcast. "I'm sorry, Kamar. I'll talk to her. Let's just enjoy the fireworks for now."

"That sounds good to me," he agreed.

They headed out to the mall parking lot and climbed the steps to be at the top of the parking garage. Most of the surface was covered with people on blankets or in folding chairs, but there were a few cars, including his pick-up truck in the corner.

"Want to get in my bed with me?" Kamar asked, pointing toward the pick-up truck.

Summer shot him a look, grinning. "I'm going to assume you mean the bed of your truck."

He laughed and nodded. "I mean, it's an open invitation for whatever you want it to be, Summer."

With his offered hand, she climbed up into the bed where he had a few cardboard boxes and a moving blanket. He placed it flat on top of the boxes to give them a softer place to sit and they settled in, their backs against the cab of the truck.

"I really am sorry," Summer repeated after a few quiet moments of staring up at the dark sky. "I don't know how to even begin to explain her behavior."

Kamar shrugged, because he honestly wasn't sure he knew what to say either. "It's...I mean, this doesn't have to happen. If I'm being honest, graduate school is pretty busy and I work most weekends playing shows. It doesn't leave a lot of time for extracurriculars. And it sounds like you're pretty busy with life—your own business, Winter. We don't have to force anything."

He wanted to put the words back in his head the moment he said them. Why had that been out loud? That was exactly the opposite of what he wanted to happen. Yeah, everything he'd said was true, but he didn't care one bit if it meant that tonight he could see where this goes. He wasn't talking about sex, but rather just connection. He hadn't felt connected to anyone in a long time, and the brief two days he'd been getting to know Summer had revived an excitement in him he had forgotten he'd lost.

"Yeah, I mean you're probably right," Summer agreed, her voice a bit quieter now.

No, I'm not right. Tell me I'm absolutely wrong.

She glanced sideways at him. "I mean, it's not like anything is happening anyway."

He lifted one brow as he caught her gaze. "I don't know if I'd say that."

The apples of her cheeks turned a light rose color that was barely perceptible under the dim parking garage lights. "I like the way you look at me."

Kamar leaned a little closer, resting his head back on the cab window and staring forward at the sky. "How do I look at you?"

"Like I'm in charge."

He wasn't expecting that answer, and he laughed in response. "Uh, what?"

Summer shook her head and leaned toward him, her arm resting on his thigh and knee. God, he loved when she touched him. "I don't mean that in a weird way—I promise. I mean, it's been a while since I've felt like I'm...I don't know, that I am me. Like, I don't know if you've noticed but I'm kind of Type A."

"I would never have guessed," he teased. Given that her hand was on his knee, he decided to be daring and reached toward her face, pushing a curl of blond hair out of her eyes and tucking it behind her ear.

Her eyes searched his for a moment, and it seemed like she wasn't even taking a breath. They were just looking into each other for the briefest of moments until she let out a soft shudder and turned her eyes back to the sky. "When I met Winter, I had just lost my mother. I felt in charge of absolutely nothing. I needed...a lot. I needed a caretaker. Grief is..."

"Absolutely horrific," he finished for her.

She nodded. "Winter liked that version of me. She hadn't met the version before my mom died, the version who built this business or put herself through college, or saved every dime she had since she was sixteen. She met the wounded part of me, and she liked it a little too much."

He wasn't exactly familiar with that circumstance, but he certainly remembered how neighbors and family members had tried to coddle him and comfort him after his mother had died. He'd basically just disappeared for a while, because he couldn't stand to let people see him that way. Instead, he'd just closed in on himself and he and his father didn't really talk about it. It was like this forbidden topic that they skirted past every day, pretending it had never happened in the first place.

"I just felt weak with Winter, and when she's around, I think I'm reminded of that part of myself," Summer finished. "She had the best of intentions. I know she meant well, but I don't like remembering that side of me."

Kamar was quiet for a few minutes, and a solitary firework shot up into the air in the distance. He watched it arch into the sky and shatter into a million golden pieces. "Can I offer another viewpoint?"

She pulled her attention from the fireworks that were now coming in steady succession and looked at him. "What do you mean?"

"When my mother died, I didn't let anyone see the wounded part of me. I just closed in on myself and...nothing. Just dealt with it alone." Kamar felt a lump in his throat as the familiar feeling of sorrow pulled at his chest. He swallowed hard. "I wish I'd been strong enough to let someone take care of me for a little while. I wish I'd been strong enough to let someone see my wounds. I wasn't strong at all, and it sounds like you were."

His last few words tangled with one another as his throat caught, and he cleared it. He could feel tears threatening, stinging at the corners of his eyes, but he blinked quickly to push them away. After all this time, and he still couldn't bring himself to show that side to anyone.

Summer didn't respond right away, but when she did, it wasn't with words. She leaned her side against his and tipped her head to lay against his shoulder. Her arm wrapped around his, hugging it to her chest and intertwining their fingers in her lap. She squeezed his hand and they both just kept looking ahead, watching the fireworks.

At least ten minutes had gone by because the fireworks were beginning to come more rapidly, and he suspected they were close to the grand finale. Summer hadn't stirred at his side, but he could feel her soft breathing as her ribs expanded and contracted against his side.

"I think it's time for the finale," he said in a hushed voice.

Summer lifted her head and looked at him. A grin stole across her lips that felt directional. "I'm ready."

There wasn't a doubt in his mind what she was talking about, and he leaned closer to her until his lips were mere breaths from hers. He only paused for a moment, just enough to remember this place and time, this feeling, the way her breath puffed against his skin like a warm embrace.

And then he closed the gap between them and pressed his lips to her.

His hand splayed across her jawline and neck, holding her to him tighter. Her fists were gripping the front of his T-shirt, doing the exact same thing. She wasn't going to let him go, and Lord knew he didn't want her to. His tongue slid across her lips and then found hers as she parted for him. Her breath quickened ever so slightly, and Kamar felt like his entire body might burst into flames right along with the fireworks still exploding in front of them.

When they pulled apart, the entire crowd on top of the

parking garage was clapping, and while he knew it was for the end of the fireworks show, it felt like it was for them. Like this was the climax of the fairytale, the moment the prince and the princess realized they were meant to be.

"Summer." He whispered her name as their foreheads pressed together and they just breathed closely to one another. "I think I can find the time."

"What?" She laughed lightly, her brows furrowing as she lifted her eyes to his.

"What I said earlier about school and work, being too busy," he repeated, shaking his head now. "Don't listen to me. That part of me that ran away when my mother died... that's who that was. That's the coward who said that. But...I don't want to keep being that person. I want to be here. Be present. Explore with you what this might be."

The corners of her lips tilted up into a small smile. "Kamar, you're not a coward."

His gaze dipped down to his hands, and he wasn't sure why those words were hitting him so hard, but he felt it in his chest. He cleared his throat and tried to focus inward for a moment. Why did it feel like he'd needed to hear that his whole life? "I appreciate that, Summer."

"And I appreciate the way you let me be all parts of myself—wounded and strong. So, I guess I have a question for you," Summer picked up his hand and traced circles across the back of it.

"What's that?" he asked.

She grinned as her eyes lifted to meet his. "Kamar, will you go out on a date with me?"

"Hell yes," he said with a laugh, shaking his head. "I'll even let you open the car door for me, Ms. Independent."

"I could be convinced," she teased, leaning into him again and placing her lips against his. Her voice softened as she pulled apart from him just enough to whisper, "Thanks for making me feel free."

The grand finale of fireworks reached a crescendo behind them and as they kissed, Kamar could see the entire sky lighting up in every color of the rainbow.

It was going to be a beautiful summer.

EPILOGUE
ONE YEAR LATER

"CONNER, what kind of cheese emergency could there possibly be?" Kamar asked, throwing his hands up as he walked briskly after the Head Cheese. "If this is another gouda cannon, I swear to God, you should have already learned your lesson last year."

The tall man shook his head and ushered him forward. "It's not the cannon—which by the way, I fixed all the glitches on that. It rains down perfect Velveeta now. I really should patent that."

Kamar laughed, but still shook his head. Somehow Conner had become one of his best friends over the last year and they were actually roommates now. He was only one summer semester away from finishing his graduate degree, and by the fall he'd be taking a teaching job in music education that had been offered by a local private school system. It was literally his dream job where he would get to build his own curriculum, had basically unlimited funds for working with the kids, and the salary was more than enough to be very comfortable.

Which was a good thing considering he wasn't just planning his own future alone anymore.

"I'm not helping you patent that," he told his friend as Conner led him up onto the rooftop of their apartment building. It was one of his favorite places because the complex had renovated it to be covered in winter-hardy succulents—basically like a green field of sustainable, energy saving efforts—but also a great way to relax in what felt like a little piece of nature in the sky. "Did the fireworks already start or something? I was going to go watch them with Summer."

He glanced at his watch, but it felt a little early for fireworks still. Usually, they were closer to nine o'clock at night because it was dark enough by then, but it was only eight thirty when Conner had caught him just as her was about to head out to Summer's place.

"Here." Conner came to a dead stop in front of the large, metal door that led out onto the rooftop. He pulled a large sparkler out from under his shirt and a lighter from his pocket.

"You just walk around with fireworks under your clothes?" Kamar asked, taking it from him and holding it still as Conner lit the top. He pushed open the door as soon as it was lit, holding the sparkler out far enough to not burn him. It crinkled loudly as it burst into flames, and he smiled, because there wasn't any adult that didn't feel that happy childhood moment when they looked at a sparkler.

"Kamar?" Summer's voice called out to him.

He looked up from the sparkler to see Summer standing in between two Adirondack chairs set out on the green. A little way behind her, Conner was jogging over to join Mara and Marco and Val and Harold as they all started lighting sparklers and waving them around in the air. Mara had an almost one-year old on her hip now and was dancing around as she showed the baby the bright lights. Saoirse, the owner of The Lucky Leprechaun, and her wife, Nell, who they'd become friends with over the last year were there as well, but instead of holding sparklers, they were both holding guitars and playing the melody of one of his songs softly.

"What is going on?" he asked, looking around at the spectacle trying to piece it altogether. "Did I miss something?"

Summer shook her head and stepped forward. "Can you come here?"

He walked over to her, still looking around them at their friends putting on quite the show. "Summer, what is going on?" he asked again.

She took a half step back from him and dropped down onto one knee. Between two fingers, she was holding a thick gold band up to him. "Kamar Jaziri, moon to my sun, will you marry me?"

It felt like everyone behind her was holding their breath, and he looked at his friends in shock. This is not at all what he'd been expecting tonight. But then he laughed and shook his head, reaching into his own pocket.

Kamar pulled out a small velvet box and flipped it open, getting down on one knee in front of Summer. "I was going to ask you that," he said, showing her the ring he'd purchased last month and had been waiting for the right moment to ask her.

There hadn't been a doubt in his mind since their first date a year ago that this was the woman he wanted to spend the rest of his life with. She pushed him to be everything he could be, and go after every dream he had. And he wanted to keep doing the same for her, even though she didn't need it. She was beyond capable all on her own, but God did he feel blessed that he got to watch her shine.

"Holy crap," Summer gasped, now looking at the gold ring with a dark black diamond set in the front. "That's beautiful!"

"So, is that a yes?" He raised his brows.

She grinned and narrowed her eyes as she waved the gold band she'd bought for him in front of him. "I asked first."

"I asked second," he teased, because he knew how much she wanted to be the one in charge right then and there and there was nothing he loved more than pressing her on that.

"On three?" she asked.

"Good Lord, is this happening or not?" Mara shouted from behind them. "It's not a competition!"

Summer laughed, and her eyes glimmered with excitement.

Harold stepped toward them and shook his head, a huge smile on his face. "I'm too old for this kind of wait. I might not make it to the actual proposal! I'm going to countdown then. Ready? Three, two, one."

At the bottom of the count, both Summer and Kamar placed the rings on one another and lifted each other to standing positions. She wrapped her arms around his neck and pressed her lips to his.

When she pulled away, he whispered to her, "I win."

"It's a tie," she replied, brushing the tip of her nose against his. "A tie for life."

"I guess I can be okay with that," he agreed. "I love you, Summer."

"I love you, Kamar. Happy Fourth of July."

He placed one more kiss on her lips. "Let freedom ring, babe."

EXCERPT FROM MALL I WANT FOR CHRISTMAS IS YOU

A HOLIDAY ROMANCE

DASH

HO HO HORRIBLE.

Dash Winters took one look at the frayed velvet red suit that the manager of Yule Heights Shopping Mall was handing him. "It's...um...it's very large."

"Oh, right." The manager turned around and reached into a metal cabinet and pulled out two yellowed pillows without any pillowcases. It was clear that they'd been white once upon a time, but now...not so much.

He grimaced at the mystery stains as the manager also handed him a thick Velcro belt. Honestly, the poor man couldn't have been older than Dash's foster father, but he spoke with a weariness that sounded ancient. "Here. Put the pillow against your stomach and wrap the band around you so it stays put. You'll look as holly jolly as any other mall Santa out there."

"Great." Dash tucked the outfit and pillow under one muscled arm and sidestepped a leak of some mystery liquid from the paneled ceiling. "So, when do I start?"

The harried manager tossed a fake white, curly beard at

Dash which he barely caught in time. "What do you mean? You start now."

"Like *now* now?" Dash had only come in for an interview, but he hadn't expected to get the job immediately. Not that he'd thought competition for mall Santa was all that intense. Especially considering his foster mother had called ahead as city councilwoman to pave the way for him.

He tucked that embarrassing thought away.

"There is already a line of kids waiting, and the Santa we've used the last few years was just arrested for driving under the influence," the manager sat down in his desk chair with a heavy thud. "I can't explain to a bunch of children that Santa drank too much milk with his cookies. So, you're it, kid."

Dash bristled slightly at the term *kid*. He was, after all, twenty-eight years old. Though he knew he had a youthful look to him, it still hit a sore spot. Probably because he had returned to living in his childhood bedroom in his foster parent's house and was now employed full-time—at least for the next twenty-five days—as a mall Santa as a favor to his mother. Despite the unfortunate turn of events his life had taken, he was trying to look at the bright side. This was all for a purpose, and, in the end, it would be worth it.

At least, that's what he hoped.

"Thanks," he replied, pulling the chord for the beard around his neck and letting it hang down like a necklace. "Is there a place I should change?"

The manager didn't even glance up from the computer he was now furiously typing away on. "The employee bathroom is at the end of the hall. The door next to the dumpsters."

Of course it was.

Dash nodded and headed out of the small office that

looked more like a converted storage closet. It had absolutely no windows and was off a concrete hallway that ran the length of the mall behind the stores. Random containers or bags of garbage were sitting outside metal doors that were marked with a store's name—most of which he recognized—but then the rest of the hallway was just empty. The off-putting lights above him was missing several bulbs and there was a buzzing sound come from a flickering bulb behind him.

He'd spent most of the last decade in Yule Heights, Michigan, after being placed with his foster parents—who he now considered just his parents—at age sixteen. He'd spent many Friday and Saturday nights loitering around this mall, but it had never occurred to him that there was an intricate behind-the-scenes set up connecting all the stores together and allowing a clear path to the garbage or parking lot without being seen by customers.

The closer he got to his destination, the stronger the smell of garbage was. A small *employee restroom* sign was hanging crookedly from one nail on the back of a door at the end of the hall, and Dash quickly made his way inside and locked it behind him after he switched on the lights.

He turned back around and surveyed the situation. The room was small enough that if he wanted to sit on the toilet and wash his hands at the same time, he certainly could. Dash hung the suit up on the back of the door, praying the rusty hook would hold. The walls were covered in crude drawings, graffiti, and flyers to someone's upcoming garage concert. He smiled slightly when he read the sloppy handwriting on the cracked mirror that said *don't hate me because I'm beautiful, hate me because I fucked your dad.* Someone else had written in another color and handwriting underneath, *go home, mom, you're drunk.*

Okay, so it wasn't all bad.

Dash made quick work of climbing out of his jeans and the ugly Christmas sweater with at least one hundred reindeer on it his mom had insisted he wear stating that it would *nail the spirit of the interview.* To be fair, she'd been right. The manager had taken one look at him and hired him on the spot.

The red pants for the Santa suit hung loosely around his legs, despite the fact that he had generally pretty thick thighs and calves. He spent one to two hours a day working out at the Planet Fitness on the other side of the mall since he didn't have much else to do with his time these days.

Another part of the reason his mother had demanded he get a job and get out of the house.

His phone started buzzing from the pocket of his discarded jeans. He fished it out and hit the answer button, accepting the video call from his older foster sister, Nell, as he propped the phone up on the bathroom sink.

"Oh, God." Nell immediately groaned through the phone. Her bright purple hair was tossed over her shoulder and he could tell from the background behind her that she was in her small kitchen apartment. She had an unusual obsession with roosters and her kitchen was decked out in cock-a-doodle-doos. "Where the hell are you? And why are you naked?"

"I have pants on." He pointed the camera down to show his bright red pants. "I'm trying to strap these pillows to my waist."

Her face scrunched up with even more confusion. "You're what?"

Dash held up his Santa hat to remind her.

Nell laughed, then took a bite of something off a large

spoon from her stove. "I forgot you were doing that. Lilian really wasn't kidding, was she?"

"Mom doesn't have a sense of humor, but she tries," Dash replied, finally getting the two pillows anchored to his stomach. He pulled the jacket overtop and attempted to button it up. "She's been asking if you're coming for Christmas Eve dinner, by the way."

"I know." Nell sighed and leaned down, propping herself up on her elbows in front of the camera. "I'm thinking about it."

"Come on, Nell. You know how much it would mean to her. Plus, none of us know what's going on with your life lately. You're like a vault." Dash pulled on the hat and adjusted his fake beard. He put out his hands in triumph. "There. Do I look like Saint Nick?"

Nell grinned and shook her head. "I'm going to need to come down to the mall sometime soon to watch you in action."

"You wouldn't dare," he threatened. "Gotta go, Nell. Christmas is calling."

She gave a quick wave and then disappeared from the screen. Dash grabbed his phone and tucked it into the waistband on his pants since he couldn't seem to find a pocket. Previous girlfriends had always complained about pants without pockets, but it wasn't until this moment that he realized how truly irritating that was.

Dash quickly tucked his previous clothes in an old grocery store bag and then left for the center of the mall. He was familiar with the Santa's Village set that was constructed in the mall's main hallway every winter, though he'd never actually participated in it before. Hell, he'd never done any sort of Santa or Christmas-themed activity until he'd moved in with the Winters. After they'd adopted him, he began to follow along with their Christmas traditions, of which there were many. The Winters did not play around when it came to holiday spirit. Their house was professional decorated, appropriately fake-snowed, and lit up bright enough to be seen the next county over.

"Santa!"

The moment Dash stepped out into the mall walkway, several little kids waved to him from behind ropes. His eyes widened as he tried to count how many children were in line, but he couldn't even see the end.

Dash waved to the crowd as a hefty, sweaty man wearing a too-tight elf costume came rushing toward him. "Uh, hello?"

"It's about time," the elf growled, grabbing the grocery bag from his hand and tossing it behind some fake presents. "Get up in your chair. Time is money, and Santa has a quota."

"He does?" Dash furrowed his brow. He was beginning to realize he should probably have asked more questions about the job to the other guy. "Oh, okay. I'll get started. What's your name?"

"Donner," the grumpy elf replied, speaking through a clenched smile that was clearly for show. "Now, let's go. I bring the kids to you, they tell you what they want. You promise them whatever they're asking for, hand them a little wrapped trinket, snap a picture for mom, and, lather, rinse, repeat."

Dash took his seat in the large red and gold throne, then waved a white-gloved hand at the line of children. Donner went to the front of the line and invited the first kid and her mother up to meet him in a sing-song voice that was clearly not his natural aggravated tone.

"Well, ho, ho, ho, young one," Dash greeted the little girl

as he helped her up onto his knee. "And what are you asking Santa for Christmas this year?"

"I want a unicorn. But it has to be rainbow." She began describing the intricate details of her unicorn dream and Dash just nodded along, chuckling. He promised her that he would see what he could do, and then they smiled for the formal photographer and for the mom who snapped a few cell phone pictures.

Next up was a slightly older boy, though he couldn't have been more than eight years old. Dash encouraged him to come on up, but the kid's feet were like concrete and he refused to move. His mother was pushing him forward, whispering harshly in his ear to *go*.

"Ho, ho, ho! Merry Christmas!" Dash greeted him once he was close enough.

The boy burst into tears and took off at a run. The mother apologized profusely and then went to chase after him.

"Rough start, Klaus." Donner shook his head and then turned a wide smile back to the crowd. "Next!"

An hour went by so fast, he hadn't even realized that he wasn't anywhere near the end of the line yet. In fact, it seemed like the line was just getting longer. Given that it was the middle of the day on a Saturday in early December, this wasn't exactly shocking.

It was, however, exhausting.

Dash enjoyed chatting with the kids about their Christmas wishes and he'd heard everything from wanting the latest Xbox to wanting parents reunited after a divorce. Despite his enjoyment, children were an incredible amount of energy. As a single man with no kids in his current life, he hadn't been fully prepared for both the volume and stickiness of this younger generation.

"Can I take a quick five?" Dash asked his elf helper between children. He glanced down at the wet candy cane stuck to his glove. "I just need to get some water. And maybe wash my hands."

Donner nodded and pulled the rope across the front of the line. "Santa's needed in his workshop! He'll be back in five minutes!"

There were a few groans from the families in line, but Dash tried not to feel guilty. He was technically only getting paid thirteen dollars an hour for this job, and he already needed a nap.

He'd move as quickly as possible, but there was no way in hell he was going back to that employee restroom by the dumpster.

Ignoring the awkward stares, Dash made his way—in full Santa gear—to the customer's bathroom off the main corridor. There was a short line of men waiting, but they were moving much quicker than the extensive line winding its way out of the ladies' room next door.

"Uh, you can go ahead of me, Santa," a young man stepped aside in line and offered him his spot.

He considered it for a moment, but he was in a rush. "Thanks, man."

"No problem. I don't want to be on your naughty list!" The young man was laughing now, and Dash rolled his eyes, but cut in front of him anyway.

After a quick visit to a stall, Dash found himself at the wide, multi-person sink trying to scrub off the candy cane now glued to his glove. A young boy came up to the sink next to him and began washing his hands, but his gaze was glued to Dash's reflection in the mirror before them.

Dash gave him a polite smile, then returned to his task.

The young boy pushed up on his tiptoes in order to turn

off the faucet. He paused and turned to face Dash. "Are you...are you Santa?"

He glanced down to see bright green eyes peeking out at him from under a thick mop of shaggy brown hair hanging low on the boy's forehead. "What?"

"Are you...um, are you Santa?"

Dash pulled his glove back on after he'd gotten off as much of the candy cane remnants off as possible. He smiled at the boy and deepened his voice. "I am. Merry Christmas!"

"My mom said we could come see you, but she's working all day," the young boy explained. "Can I tell you what I want for Christmas even though we're in a bathroom?"

Another man walked past them to the open sink, side-eying him. Dash cleared his throat and then got down on one knee. "Sure, kid. What's your name?"

"I'm Rudy." The boy beamed and straightened, standing taller. "Last year, you got me a model-making kit. I made a replica of the Eiffel Tower."

"That's pretty cool," Dash replied, chuckling and giving his best *ho ho ho* in the throaty laugh. "How'd it turn out?"

"Great! I love it! I still play with it," Rudy confessed. He was fidgeting with his hands now. "But, this year, can I ask for something for my mom?"

Dash tilted his head to the side. He smiled at the sweet concern on the boy's face. "Well, sure. Moms need Christmas gifts, too."

Rudy nodded. "I made her a picture with my teacher, too."

"Great job," Dash replied.

The boy stepped a little closer and lowered his voice slightly. "I was hoping you could teach my mom how to drive a sleigh."

He paused, considering the strange request. "You want me to teach your mom how to drive a sleigh?"

"She's *terrible* at driving," Rudy continued. "And she said that's why we don't have a car. But sleighs are harder to drive than cars, right? So, maybe if she learns how to drive a sleigh, then she can drive a car!"

"That is...well, that is some sound logic, son," Dash said with a laugh. "I can see this is important to you."

"It is," Rudy agreed. "I don't want to keep taking the bus everywhere. It's so smelly, and we have to get up so early to make it across town for her shift on weekends. I know she says it's fine, but I can tell she hates it, too."

Dash felt a thump in his chest as he pictured this little boy on a bus every weekend accompanying his mom to work. He certainly wasn't a stranger to buses. Hell, he'd spent most of his childhood using that as his sole means of transportation. Since finding the Winters, however, his life had changed dramatically. He had been gifted a car that he loved and refused to get rid of even years later when it had certainly seen better days. "Uh, so...where's your mom, kid?"

"I'll bring you to her!" Rudy grabbed his gloved hand and started pulling him toward the door. "Then you can tell her in person!"

Dash allowed himself to be led away, trying to figure out how he'd explain to Donner that he was teaching someone to drive a sleigh on his short bathroom break.

Well, won't that be awkward.

Live on All Retailers

EXCERPT FROM MISADVENTURES IN THE CAGE

A MISADVENTURES ROMANCE

CHAPTER ONE

"Oh my God...Josie? Josie Gray?" A young African American woman with short black hair and a vibrantly metallic dress on sidled up to her at the bar. "Can I please get a picture with you?"

Josie shot back the glass of tequila and then sucked on the lime, hissing as it hit her stomach hard. She was already four shots in and each one was helping her forget the giant rejection letter she was carrying around in her purse.

We regret to inform you that the position of sous chef is no longer available blah blah blah.

She got the point. She was never going to be a chef. Every job application she'd sent in over the last year had been turned down.

Not that she was even allowed to be one anyway.

"Sure," she replied, finally turning to the woman and putting on her best fake smile.

The woman held up her iPhone, turning the camera around to face them and put on her best duck face as she posed for the camera next to Josie.

Josie just smiled and then turned back to the bar as soon as the photo was done.

"Another one," she indicated to the bartender, but when she lifted her hand to motion, she knocked over her glass. Thankfully, it didn't shatter, but it made a loud ass noise as it clattered against the bar.

The bartender shook his head, casting her a pitying look. God, she hated that. "Miss Gray, I think you've had enough. Why don't I call you a cab?"

"No," she sighed loudly. Admittedly, she was getting tired and had probably had enough. Plus, she couldn't really afford TMZ to find her and write an article about how the reality television star was wasted and falling all over herself at a local bar. Hell, it was the entire reason she'd come to this place off the strip to begin with—anonymity. So much for that. "I'll order a Lyft. Thank you, though."

She paid her check and then pulled out her phone, ordering a ride through the ride share app. Honestly, she wasn't normally like this. She didn't regularly go get drunk by herself at a bar off the Las Vegas strip in a seedy part of town.

Hell, this entire town was a seedy part of town depending on how you looked at it.

She'd spent her entire life living in Las Vegas though, so it was home to her. She was comfortable with its antics and qualms. Something about it...she could handle. At least, that's what she told herself.

Pulling her sweater up around her shoulders, she grabbed her purse and decided to wait for her Lyft out front. She could really use the still, night air to sober up before getting in a lurching car ride. God forbid she puke in the back of someone else's car.

She debated canceling the Lyft and just calling her

driver, but then he would tell her brother where she'd been and she'd never hear the end of it. No, she needed the time off the clock and away from the freaking cameras.

"Hey, Miss," a voice called out to her as she stood on the front steps of the bar trying to take some deep breaths. "You left this on the bar."

She turned to see an older gentleman, maybe twenty years her senior, approaching her. He was holding a tube of lipstick. She didn't recognize it and it certainly wasn't hers. She never wore lipstick.

She shook her head. "That's not mine."

"Are you sure?" He frowned, then glanced back up at her. "I bet it would look real pretty on your chocolate skin."

Josie pulled her sweater tighter around her, hoping the Lyft decided to show up sooner rather than later. "It's not mine," she repeated.

"Why don't you try it on?" he insisted. "Let's just test it out."

"No." She moved away from him, but he approached her faster.

"Just try it on, sweet thing." He grabbed her wrist and twisted it, yanking her backward. "I just want to see how it looks on ya."

"Let go of me!" she yelled, struggling to free her arm from his grasps.

"Don't be such an uppity little bitch," the older man said, squeezing her wrist tighter and tighter until she cried out in pain. "I've seen you on TV before."

"Hey!" A fist came out of nowhere and landed squarely against the older man's jaw.

He staggered back, releasing Josie's wrist and clutching his bruising face. "What the hell?"

"The lady said let go," the owner of the fist—a tall, buff

young man who looked like a brick wall stuffed in a suit—instructed her attacker. "I suggest you listen to women when they talk. I'd also suggest you leave and not come back. Now."

The older man scurried away like a dog with his tail between his legs. She wasn't sorry to see him go.

The newcomer turned back to her, concern etched on his features as his brows furrowed. "Are you okay?"

"I...I think so?" She got back up to her feet and examined her wrist, wincing at the pain.

He noticed her expression right away. "We need to get you to a hospital."

"No way," she opposed the idea right away. "I'm not spending all night in a hospital room when I know it's not broken. It just needs some ice probably."

Plus, she couldn't afford the fall out from the media over yet another family scandal. It was bad enough that her entire family was on a reality television show thanks to her brother's career that chronicled her every move, but knowing that any little thing she did could be used as fodder for an episode was a nightmare waiting to happen.

"See, I can still move it?" She gingerly moved her wrist.

A small smirk played across his lips and she couldn't help but notice a slight Irish accent to his words. "Useful."

"Thank you for your help," she stammered, trying to find something to say to this incredibly gorgeous man who'd just rode in like Prince Charming and saved her life. "I'll just go find my Lyft now."

"What's your name?" he asked, seeming to ignore everything she just said.

"Josie." It was a nice change of pace to run into someone who didn't know who she was. Although, that wasn't very unusual with men because they weren't really the target demographic for her family's show.

He nodded. "I'm Callan."

"Nice to meet you, Callan." She started to walk away again, but he interrupted her again.

"Need a ride home?" he asked, motioning to his car parked against the curb. Of course, it had to be a freaking Range Rover. She wondered who the hell was this guy. It certainly wasn't unusual in Las Vegas to run in to celebrities, but she didn't recognize him...although something about his face...he did look familiar.

She glanced down at her phone and checked her Lyft app. Her driver was still thirteen minutes away. *What the hell?* She canceled the ride. "Sure? Why not."

A ride with a life-saving, potential celebrity sounded safer anyway than with a total stranger vetted only by an app. At least, that's the story she was going to tell herself to convince herself to get into the car with this drop dead handsome man. And when she said drop dead handsome, she meant it. The dude was gawking-worthy. Chiseled muscles on every inch of his body that she could see. Long, brown wavy hair tied back in a pony tail, and blue eyes that made her knees feel like they were made of jello.

"Is this your car?" she asked, motioning to the Range Rover.

He nodded and opened the passenger door for her. "Hop in."

"Hold on. One second." She walked around to the front of the car and took a picture of the car and license plate and sent it off in a quick text to her best friend, Emily.

"Did you just take a picture of my license plate?" he asked, one brow raised as he watched her.

"And texted it to my friend," she confirmed, waltzing past him and climbing into the passenger seat of the car.

He chuckled, leaning against the door frame. "Can I ask why?"

"In case you murder me, obviously." She turned to face him, giving him a deadpan expression like it was the most obvious thing ever. Honestly, it was. Her mother had taught her that trick years ago, and you learn a thing or two growing up in Las Vegas. Men are a lot less likely to act nefariously when they know they're being held accountable by an anonymous third party.

A grin spread wide across his face and it only made his beautiful features all the more glorious. "Smart lady." He closed her car door and she watched as he walked around the car and then climbed into the driver's seat. "Where to, Ms. Precaution?"

Maybe it was the tequila talking, or maybe it was the fact that he was daring her to throw caution to the wind, or maybe she was just fed up with the monotony of her life and wanted to throw a wrench at things. She wasn't sure what made the next words come out of her mouth. All she knew was that she said them and she didn't want to take them back...and thank God, she didn't.

"Take me to your place."

Live on All Retailers

ABOUT THE AUTHOR

Contemporary Romances Across the Rainbow

Sarah Robinson first started her writing career as a published poet in high school, and then continued in college, winning several poetry awards and being published in multiple local literary journals.

Never expecting to make a career of it, a freelance writing Craigslist job accidentally introduced her to the world of book publishing. Lengthening her writing from poetry to novels, Robinson published her first book through a small press publisher, before moving into self-publishing, and then finally accepting a contract from Penguin Random House two years later. She continues to publish both traditionally and indie with over 18+ novels to her name with publishers like Penguin, Waterhouse Press, Hachette, and more. She has achieved awards and accolades including 2021 Vivian Award Finalist, Top 10 iBooks Bestseller, Top 25 Amazon Kindle Bestseller, and Top 5 Barnes & Noble Bestseller. She has been published in three languages.

In her personal life, Sarah Robinson is happily married to the gentle giant of her dreams and one rambunctious toddler. They have a home full of love, snuggly pets, and are happily living in Arlington, Virginia.

Did You Enjoy This Novella? Leave a Review!

You can help the author by **leaving a review**! Reviews on the online book retailer where you purchased this novella help the author so much!

I Want To Do More! How Else Can I Help?

If you want to get even more involved and help the author, you can follow Sarah on social media and interact online! You can join Sarah's Facebook Reader Group (*Robinson's Ramblings*) and/or her newsletter! You can also follow any of her social media sites below!

Follow the Author on Social Media

booksbysarahrobinson.com
subscribepage.com/sarahrobinsonnewsletter
facebook.com/booksbysarahrobinson
twitter.com/booksby_sarah
goodreads.com/booksbysarahrobinson
instagram.com/booksbysarahrobinson

ALSO BY SARAH ROBINSON

The Photographer Trilogy

(Romantic Suspense)

Tainted Bodies

Tainted Pictures

Untainted

Forbidden Rockers Series

(Rockstar Romances)

Logan's Story: A Prequel Novella

Her Forbidden Rockstar

Rocker Christmas: A Logan & Caroline Holiday Novella

Kavanagh Legends Series

(MMA Fighter Standalone Romances)

Breaking a Legend

Saving a Legend

Becoming a Legend

Chasing a Legend

Kavanagh Christmas

Nudes Series

(Hollywood Standalone Romances)

NUDES

BARE

SHEER

At the Mall Series

(Romantic Comedy Shorts)

Mall I Want for Christmas is You

Mall You Need is Love

Mall Out of Luck

Mall American Girl

More coming soon...

Heart Lake Series

(Small Town Romances)

Dreaming of a Heart Lake Christmas (Coming September 2022)

Little Bookstore on Heart Lake Lane (Coming 2023)

Standalone Novels

Not a Hero: A Bad Boy Marine Romance

Misadventures in the Cage

One Night Stand Serial

Second Shot of Whiskey

Women's Fiction

Every Last Drop